D0496096

The Quest for the Vest

Maverick

Chapter Readers

'The Quest for the Vest'
An original concept by Jenny Jinks
© Jenny Jinks 2021

Illustrated by Claudio Cerri

Published by MAVERICK ARTS PUBLISHING LTD

Studio 11, City Business Centre, 6 Brighton Road,

Horsham, West Sussex, RH13 5BB

© Maverick Arts Publishing Limited November 2021

+44 (0)1403 256941

A CIP catalogue record for this book is available at the British Library.

ISBN 978-1-84886-838-0

www.maverickbooks.co.uk

This book is rated as: Lime Band (Guided Reading)

The Quest for the Vest

Written by
Jenny Jinks

Illustrated by
Claudio Cerri

Chapter 1

Gus sighed. It was only a few days until his birthday. Normally he would be jumping with excitement, but not this year. Because this year, it was Gus's turn to be sent on a quest.

It was tradition. Everyone in Gus's family had to go on a quest.

Great Uncle Magnus defended the kingdom from a family of dragons.

Grandma Suki stopped an erupting volcano from destroying the valley.

Gus's own brother found the Lost Crystal of the Forbidden Forest, and brought luck to the whole kingdom!

It was a great honour to be sent on a quest, and most people looked forward to it. But Gus had a secret. He didn't like adventure. He didn't like danger. And he especially didn't like quests.

Gus couldn't tell his parents, of course. They would be so disappointed. So Gus pretended to be excited, while inside he felt sick with worry.

Gus's father sighed. It was only a few days until

Gus's birthday. But Gus's father had a secret. He did not have a quest for Gus. Since Gus's brother had brought luck to the kingdom, there was nothing left to do! He couldn't tell Gus this, of course. He would be so disappointed. So he pretended to be excited for Gus, while inside he felt sick with worry.

Chapter 2

The morning of Gus's birthday finally arrived.

Gus dragged himself downstairs to find his whole

family waiting for him.

"Today is the big day. Quest day!" Grandma Suki said, giving Gus a squeeze. Gus forced a smile. "Well, don't leave the poor boy waiting," she said to Gus's father. "What is his quest?"

"Well," said Gus's father, thinking quickly. "It's a quest for..." Everyone leaned in close. He glanced around in desperation. The porridge bubbled on the stove, the washing hung on the line. That was it! **"A VEST!"**

"A... vest?!" everyone cried.

"Yes!" Gus's father said. "The Quest for the Vest! You must find the strongest silk to make the best protective vest the kingdom has ever seen! Off you go, my boy. Not a moment to lose. Your people are depending on you!"

And with that, Gus's father pushed him out of the door and waved him on his way.

Chapter 3

Gus hadn't got very far before he felt homesick.

Or maybe he was just hungry. His tummy gave a

loud rumble. He hadn't even had time to eat his

birthday breakfast. He looked through his bag for

something to eat but he only had a skipping rope.

What good was that? Gus threw the bag on the

ground.

"Hey!" said a voice, and a rabbit poked its head up from the long grass.

"Oh, sorry," said Gus. "I didn't know anyone was there."

The rabbit hopped over to sit next to Gus.

Gus had never met a rabbit before. His eldest

brother's quest was to chase all the rabbits out

of the kingdom. They were pests that ruined the

harvest. But it looked as if this one had escaped.

"My name is Snuff. You don't look very happy.

Are you alright?"

Gus shrugged.

"Have you lost your family?" asked Snuff.

"I've lost mine. I'm looking for them. They used

to live round here. Maybe we could look for our

families together!"

"I know where my family is," said Gus. "They're just not here. I'm on my own. I'm on a quest."

"A quest? That sounds very important," Snuff said. "What's a quest?"

Gus explained about his quest for the vest.

"Oooh, how exciting! But why would you want to do it on your own? Everything is better with friends!" Snuff sniffed. "I know! I can help you look for your silk, and you can help me look for my family."

Gus thought for a moment. There was no rule that he *had* to do it by himself.

"Okay, you can come."

"You won't even know I'm here!" Snuff said,

jumping about excitedly. He landed on Gus's foot.

Gus wondered if he had made a massive mistake.

Chapter 4

Having Snuff around was actually quite nice.

He knew more about the wild than Gus did, and

found them fresh water and berries when it was

time for lunch.

And Snuff's constant chatter stopped Gus worrying about his quest.

Snuff was just telling Gus a story about one of his many brothers when he stopped suddenly. Gus walked right into the back of him.

"Did you hear that?" asked Snuff, one ear raised.

Gus couldn't hear anything.

Snuff turned away from the path and hopped off. Gus decided he had better follow him, just in case Snuff got into any trouble. Before long they came to a well. A low moaning was coming from deep inside.

"Snuff, careful!" Gus hissed as Snuff hopped straight over to the well.

"Who's down there?" Snuff called. A deep grunt answered. Snuff hopped back to Gus, shaking his head. "Oh dear. Big trouble."

"What is it?" Gus asked.

"A troll!" said Snuff.

"A troll?" cried Gus. "Quick, let's run!"

Chapter 5

Snuff didn't move.

"Why aren't you running?" Gus asked. He had heard about trolls. His great-great-grandfather was nearly eaten by one on his quest. They were big and mean, and would eat you if you got too close.

"We can't go!" said Snuff. "The troll is in big trouble! We must help him!"

"But... what if he eats us?"

"Eat us?" Snuff sniffed. "Everyone knows that trolls are vegetarian."

Gus paused. Vegetarian? But what about his great-great-grandfather?

"Are you sure?" Gus asked.

"Oh yes, definitely," said Snuff.

"Okay," said Gus hesitantly. "I might have something that will help."

Gus pulled out the skipping rope. They tied one end round a tree and lowered the other end down the well. They pulled and pulled. Finally the troll's head appeared over the top of the well and he heaved himself out.

"GAAAAAAARRRRRRR,"

roared the troll angrily.

Gus got ready to run. But Snuff hopped right over to him and began chatting away to the troll.

"This is Brock. He's a mountain troll," Snuff told Gus. "He's been trapped down that well for ages. It's good we came along when we did. I told Brock about your quest. He knows where to find the strongest silk in the world!"

"Garumph," grunted Brock.

"He says he will take us there, as a thank you for rescuing him," Snuff said.

"You understood that?" Gus said.

"Of course," nodded Snuff.

Gus wasn't sure whether they could trust Brock. Until now, Gus had always thought that rabbits were pests and trolls were dangerous. But he was beginning to wonder if anything he had been told was true.

"Okay," said Gus.

So they set off together, with Brock leading the way.

Chapter 6

Having Brock with them was quite helpful.

He lifted them over a huge fallen tree, and

carried Snuff when his little legs got tired.

Gus had forgotten all about his quest, until they suddenly stopped in the middle of nowhere.

"Garumph," Brock said.

"We're here," translated Snuff.

"Where?" asked Gus. There was nothing but mountains.

Brock pointed to a hole in the side of the mountain. A cave.

"Brock says you will find what you are looking for inside that cave," Snuff said.

Gus and Snuff peered inside. It was very dark. Even Snuff looked afraid. One of Gus's long lost relatives had gone on a quest to a cave.

They had never returned. Caves were dark, and full of scary beasts.

Or at least, he thought they were.

"Wait here. This is my quest. I'm not putting you in any danger," Gus said, much more bravely than he felt.

"I won't leave my friend," said Snuff, and he added in a whisper, "Brock will stay out here. He spent too long down that well. I think he is scared of small, dark spaces now."

"Oh," said Gus. He felt a little less brave, knowing that big strong Brock wouldn't be with them.

But Snuff took his hand, and together they

stepped into the dark cave.

Chapter 7

Once Gus's eyes got used to the dark, the cave wasn't that scary after all. There were shiny rocks, little pools and amazing creatures he had never seen before. It was beautiful. But there was no sign of anything you could use to make a vest. Perhaps Brock had got it wrong. Gus was just investigating some rock pools when he heard a shriek. Snuff!

Gus found Snuff caught in some sticky string.

"Don't worry, I'll get you down," Gus said.

But the sticky threads were too strong, and Gus got caught in them too. Now they were both stuck.

"HELP!" they shouted at the top of their lungs.

Finally they heard the thud of footsteps.

"Over here!" Gus cried.

But then he saw something big, with long hairy legs, coming closer and closer. It stopped right in front of them and peered at them with its eight big shiny eyes. A huge, hairy spider!

"Aaaaaaah!"

Chapter 8

It took Gus a moment to realise that he wasn't the one shouting. The spider was screaming at the top of her lungs.

"It's okay," Gus called out. "We won't hurt you."

Suddenly, a second set of footsteps echoed through the cave, and Gus saw the big friendly face of...

"Brock! You came!" Gus cried happily. "We're stuck, and this spider won't stop screaming."

When the spider heard Brock's name, she stopped and looked up.

"Brock?" she said. "Is it really you?!"

Brock spoke to the spider, and she quickly got to work freeing Gus and Snuff.

"I'm sorry you got stuck in my web," the spider said.

"This is your web?" said Gus, looking at the silk in his hands thoughtfully.

"Yes, it's such a pain. Terrible stuff to get caught in. Never met anyone else who can break it. Not that anybody comes here. I haven't seen another soul since Brock moved away years ago, so I'm a bit nervous of strangers."

"But we're friends of Brock! And that means we're your friends too!" Snuff said kindly. "You should join us. We're on a very important quest. Tell her about your quest, Gus!"

But Gus was silent.

"We're looking for some super strong silk to make a very important vest," Snuff continued. "Something that can't be broken! You know, like..." Snuff looked at Gus and the silk in his hands. "The silk! You found the silk!"

Chapter 9

Gus had found the strongest silk, alright. It was exactly what he was looking for. Brock knitted a beautiful vest out of the silk that the spider had given him. Who knew that cave trolls were so good at knitting?!

Meanwhile, Snuff told them stories about his many brothers and sisters. Gus looked round at the group. Soon the vest would be done. Then he could take it home and complete his quest. But

Gus didn't want to go home. He wasn't ready for

his adventure to be over. And he didn't want to

leave his friends.

Finally Brock had finished the vest.

It really was the finest vest Gus had ever seen.

"Grumpher," Gus said (which Snuff had taught him was 'thank you' in Troll).

Brock looked delighted, and scooped Gus up into a rib-crushing hug.

"Your quest is complete!" Snuff said. "Your family will be so proud."

Gus's face suddenly lit up.

"Family! That's it! I *haven't* finished my quest!" said Gus. "I promised to help you find your family. I can't go home yet. My quest isn't complete!"

Snuff grinned. "You'll really help me still?"

"Of course I will," said Gus. "And if we can't find them, then you'll always have me and Brock."

"Well then, what are we waiting for?" said Snuff, hopping up and down excitedly. "We've got a quest to complete."

Discussion Points

1. What was Gus's dad's secret at the beginning of the story?

2. Who was stuck down the well?
a) Gus
b) Brock
c) Snuff's family

3. What was your favourite part of the story?

4. Where did Gus find the super strong silk?

5. Why do you think Gus didn't want to go on a quest?

6. Who was your favourite character and why?

7. There were moments in the story when Gus had to be **brave**. Where do you think the story shows this most?

8. What do you think happens after the end of the story?

Book Bands for Guided Reading

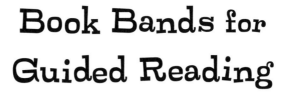

The Institute of Education book banding system is a scale of colours that reflects the various levels of reading difficulty. The bands are assigned by taking into account the content, the language style, the layout and phonics. Word, phrase and sentence level work is also taken into consideration.

The Maverick Readers Scheme is a bright, attractive range of books covering the pink to grey bands. All of these books have been book banded for guided reading to the industry standard and edited by a leading educational consultant.

To view the whole Maverick Readers scheme, visit our website at

www.maverickearlyreaders.com

Or scan the QR code to view our scheme instantly!

Pink
Red
Yellow
Blue
Green
Orange
Turquoise
Purple
Gold
White
Lime
Brown
Grey

Maverick Chapter Readers
(From Lime to Grey Band)